Show Me the Honey

SHOW ME THE HONEY
A BANTAM BOOK 978 0 857 51353 3

Published in Great Britain by Bantam,
an imprint of Random House Children's Publishers UK
A Random House Group Company

This edition published 2011

Bantam Books are published by Random House Children's Publishers UK,
61–63 Uxbridge Road, London W5 5SA

www.**seussville**.com
www.**randomhousechildrens**.co.uk

Addresses for companies within The Random House Group Limited can be found at:
www.randomhouse.co.uk/offices.htm

THE RANDOM HOUSE GROUP Limited Reg. No. 954009

A CIP catalogue record for this book is available from the British Library

Printed in China

Show Me the Honey

By Tish Rabe

From a script by Ken Cuperus

Illustrated by Christopher Moroney

BANTAM BOOKS

"This morning," said Nick,
"I'd like honey on toast.
That is the breakfast that
I like the most!"
"Me too," said Sally,
"but I'm sorry to say,
it looks like we're all
out of honey today."

4

"Sally," Nick said,
"your joke isn't funny.
I can't eat my breakfast
if we're out of honey!"

"Did someone say 'honey'?"
cried the Cat. "What a treat!
It's gloppy and sloppy
and sticky and sweet.
I love it on pancakes,
all fluffy and hot.
Please pour me a bit
of the honey you've got!"

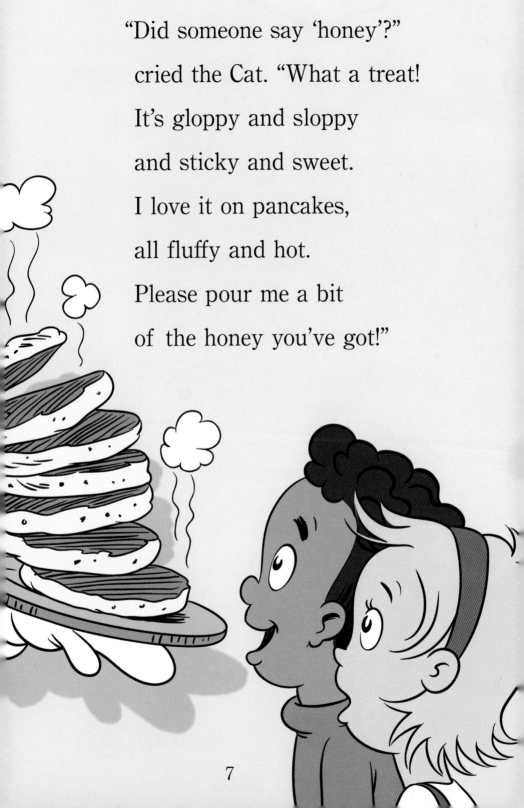

"It's all gone," said Nick.

"Is there some in your hat?"

"Oh dear . . . ," said the Cat.

"No, I do not have that.

But I have something else –

a Special Invitation

to Queen Priscilla Buzzoo's

Dance-All-Day Celebration!

She is queen of the bees

and her parties are great.

But we've got to hurry

or we will be late!"

"There's one problem," said Sally.
"Look here and you'll see –
to go to the party
you must be a bee."

Queen Priscilla Buzzoo's
Dance-All-Day Celebration
Meet at the hive
at a quarter past five.
(Bees only, please.)

"Don't worry," the Cat said.

"I know what to do.

This is a job for

Thing One and Thing Two!"

12

So the two Things ran in and
the Cat asked them, "Please,
do something to make us
fit in with the bees."

In a flash those two Things,
with their usual knack,
striped the kids and the Cat
with yellow and black.

"I can't believe it," said Nick.

"I look just like a bee.

   This is something that I

   never thought I would see!"

"We're off!" said the Cat.
"We will meet Queen Buzzoo.
We'll meet her and greet her
and dance with her too!
Push the Shrinkamadoodle
if you would, please.
It will shrink us down to
the size of the bees."

"We'll fly past the ladybugs
and wave to the birds,
who will sing us some songs
that don't have any words.
We will soar and, what's more,
we will dip and we'll dive
through a hole in a tree
and down into the hive."

18

They got to the party
a few minutes late
and were stopped by two bees
who were guarding the gate.
"Excuse me," one said.
"Where is your invitation
to Queen Priscilla Buzzoo's
Dance-All-Day Celebration?"
"Here it is!" Sally said.
The bees said, "Go in!
The special bee dance
is about to begin!"

"Nick and Sally," the Cat said,
"let me introduce you
   to the queen of the bees,
   Queen Priscilla Buzzoo."
"Hello," said the queen.
"Welcome to my hive.
   My party just started
   at a quarter past five."
"Your Beeness," Nick said,
"I'd like to thank you.
   This is the first party
   of bees I've been to!"

Then they heard buzzing,
and in front of the throne
one worker bee started
to dance all alone!
She zigged and she zagged,
then she wiggled
and waggled.

She slipped and she slid
and she jiggled and jaggled.
She swirled and she twirled
with a buzz and a spin,
and then . . .

. . . more and more bees
began to join in!

Soon all the bees were
dancing and twirling.
Wings and antennae
were swinging and swirling.
Then Sally and Nick
began to dance too.
"Bee-utiful!" cried
Queen Priscilla Buzzoo.

"Watch the bees!" said the Cat.
"And you'll get a surprise –
they aren't just dancing
to get exercise!"

"The first bee that danced,"
Sally said, "let me guess.
She was showing them something."
The Cat cried out, "Yes!"

"Her dance showed something bees need to survive – where to find nectar to bring to the hive. They get nectar from flowers. It's sticky and sweet. They use it to make the sweet honey they eat."

33

"Her special bee dance
lets the other bees know
where to find flowers
and which way to go."

"Can we help them?" asked Sally.

The Cat said, "Indeed!

We can follow and help them

find nectar they need."

35

"To the Thinga-ma-jigger!

Get ready to fly.

Hold on to your hats

and we'll take to the sky!"

"Let's go!" said Nick.

"If we hurry, we'll see

how bees make honey.

How hard could it be?"

So they flew with the bees
and slurped nectar from flowers,
then returned to the hive
in a couple of hours.

At the hive they spit nectar
into combs, where it dried.
Soon all of those combs
had sweet honey inside.

"In these combs," the queen said,

"we store honey away."

"This is fun!" Sally cried.

"I could do this all day."

41

"Next, we must cover
the combs," said the queen.
"This protects the honey
and helps keep it clean."
"I like honey," said Nick.
"I like honey a lot.
But making it is much
more work than I thought!"

"It's late," said the Cat,

"and it's time we must go,

but we'll come back to visit

you all soon, I know."

"So long!" buzzed the bees.

"And be sure to come back

anytime you want honey

to eat for a snack."

Back home they all opened
their gifts from the queen –
more jars of honey than
they'd ever seen!
"The note says," said Sally,
"'We want to give you
the world's sweetest honey,
from the Hive of Buzzoo.'"

"I liked meeting the queen
and flying through trees.
But what I liked most,"
Nick said . . .

"... was dancing with bees!"